Alumni

Fund

Alumni Fund

CHRISTOPHER LEE BOWEN

ARPress
45 Dan Road Suite 5
Canton, MA 02021

Hotline: 1(888) 821-0229
Fax: 1(508) 545-7580

Ordering Information:
Quantity sales. Special discounts are available on quantity purchases by corporations, associations, and others. For details, contact the publisher at the address above.

Printed in the United States of America.

ISBN-13:   Softcover
            eBook   979-8-89330-390-2
            Hardback   979-8-89330-391-9

Library of Congress Control Number: 2024903100

Alumni Fund

Amelia Abernathy, small, thin, blue-rinsed hair, watery green eyes, patrician, in her late 70's, walked onto the balcony of her 16th story penthouse overlooking Central Park wearing a green gardening apron, humming, smiling a vacant dementia smile, hand eye coordination unreliable, faculties in decline. Memory disordered so that current, recent, even fairly distant memories fade and long-past college days reclaim prominence, as she listens to the alumni fund donor bonus CD of the Abington College 'hymn' (an amalgam of *My Country 'Tis of Thee*, *Brigadoon* and the *Ghana National Anthem*) received recently and played repeatedly. The beloved words sung by the Bennington glee club, in her time entirely soprano, now (after going coed four years ago) muddied by baritone undertones.

> *A-bing-ton, Al-ma ma-ter*
> *Standing un-der state-ly trees…*

She goes over to geraniums set it in boxes around the periphery of the balcony, sits on her heels and digs with a small trowel. In the distance, the assertive skyline of New York under a clear blue sky.

> *…We'll re-main your loyal daugh-ters*
> *All our hearts are pledged to thee…..*

Behind her a stocky figure appears in faded green utility overalls and commercial cap. On the back of his jacket are the words Manhattan Maintenance Services.

Gently, quickly, firmly he lifts Amelia like a basket and drops her over the side of the balcony.

....We'll not forget the tears and laughter
While glad-ness lives in memory....

The chorus swells to the final verse of the college hymn as she drops out of sight. Her bewildered smile, the last thing he sees as he waves good bye, the red ruby gold ring on his little finger the last thing to catch her eye.

....What e'er may hap here-af-ter, Al-ma Ma-ter.
All our hearts are pledged to thee.

Abington is a venerable if somewhat worn Vermont women's college, now co-educational. Bright white student dorms, blue shutters, multi-paned windows, brick academic buildings with slate roofs and white steeples, in a setting of red, yellow October leaves, blue sky, white clouds, crisp apple-scented air, create an impression of academic order, enterprise and diligence. An impression Jessica Hyde confirms, dressed in a Brooks Brothers tweed suit, white blouse, cameo at the collar, practical but stylish shoes, as she parks a new cobalt blue Jaguar convertible and crosses campus toward the Administration building.

Abington College founder, Melanie Sprout, née Livingston, as if nodding approval, stands bronzed in a bestowing gesture on a marble plinth at the far end of the commons. At a distance, Abington College appears nearly unchanged from its founding in 1837. Close up, not so much. Groups of students slouch on the commons, a pervasive slackness suggesting latter-day erosion of past standards of dress and demeanor. Bare feet, bra-less, cut-off jeans, orange-dyed hair, nose rings, the usual suspects. Jessica passes a huddle of students surrounding a Black professor in African shirt, who pounds several goat-hide drums of different sizes as the students hump around to the beat.

She walks up the steps of the Administration Building, through the large oak door above which, engraved in the granite arch, is the College motto: LUX NIHIL FORTIOR. Pascal du Pin sur Roche, head of the French department, his blue beret and red neck scarf adding Gallic flair, waves from a bank of long leather sofas inside the main hall where a dozen students drink coffee, read mail, nibble doughnuts. Jessica waves back, turns left toward the mail room, takes a bundle of mail from the open box marked Alumni Fund Staff, heads up the worn stone stairs and enters her office on the second floor.

A roll top desk and file cabinets stacked with alumni bulletins, letters, manila folders, photos in different sized frames hang on the walls--graduating classes, award ceremonies, autographed photos of former faculty and Presidents of Abington. Louise, her clerical assistant, hands Jessica alumni folders for this afternoon's trip to New York. Jessica looks through the list of names, class year, current year annual fund contributions, total lifetime contributions, LIVING TRUST amount. The generosity profile of dedicated alumna in the Big Apple, with a stapled note that yesterday $3.4 million was transferred electronically to the Alumni Fund from the estate of Amelia Abernathy.

Have to run Louise, board meeting. Would you please confirm my flight to New York?

ANOTHER UNISEX BATHROOM FOR A DEMOCRATIC SOCIETY stenciled on the opaque glass of the restroom door down the hall from the boardroom serves as a reminder of progressive changes made on campus over the last two years. Sharp words come from within, as the door opens abruptly, and Marjorie Weatherby emerges. About 50, platinum hair, tight facelift, rich clothes. She is attractive but her arrogant, peevish expression makes that hard to notice. Just before the door closes, we see behind her two students, just interrupted in a questionable activity by Marjorie, evident provocation for her outraged expression.

Well really! I have never in my life…

Furious and red-faced Marjorie walks briskly down the hall and enters the Abington College Board room, mahogany-paneled, leaded glass windows, long oak table and high-backed leather chairs. Board members gathered in small groupings, looking displeased, muttering misgivings, some seated, some standing, all impatient. Leonard Abernathy and Eleanor Mason are seated in rapt confidential discussion, their place cards clearly identify them.

Terrible news of course. But poor Amelia had become so…so absent minded lately…I suppose she lost her balance…she did love her flowers so….

In their 70's, wealthy, arthritic, a necessarily subdued but unmistakable erotic connection developing.

College President Sarah Goldrock, stocky, butch, in olive-drab jumpsuit amply provided with zipper pockets and grenade rings, stands at parade rest at one end of the table. She exaggerates her tough Bronx accent at board meetings, rather than glossing over her incongruous presence as President of this prestigious *haute bourgeoise* college. The dozen trustees shift uneasily and exchange meaningful looks or turn occasionally to whisper something to their neighbor, creating an overall impression of being at bay, even besieged.

If you all sit down, we can get started. Welcome to the quarterly Board Meeting. As we begin a new academic year, I think we can afford to toot our horn a little. In fact, I can say that academically we are on a roll. The African Music division has received three grants from the National Foundation for Affirmative Action thanks to the work of Professor Akimba Toomumba on drum signals among West African crocodile societies.

Venable Sprout, great great great grandson of the college founder, snorts audibly into his coffee mug an irrepressible eructation prompted by the latest denigration of former standards, Bronx terrorist and African intrusions, that have brought Abington, his GGG grandmother's vision of sisterly perfection, so visibly and audibly low.

The Gay Rights Foundation awarded a three-year grant for my Special Studies Seminar on Lesbianism in American Literature. In addition, the Trust for Political Activism recognized our Political Science division with a cash award for the most active demonstration program for a college of less than 2000 students.

Board Chair Marjorie Weatherby smiles acidly at Leonard Abernathy, his responding smirk and raised eyebrows confirming his like reaction to this travesty.

We have definitely improved the financial situation of the college as well. For that, of course we owe so much to Jessica Hyde and her remarkable work with the Alumni Fund these past three years. Jessica will give you an update on the Alumni Fund.

Board member pouts turn to smiles at the mention of Jessica, who smiling modestly, rises, fumbles with a few papers, twinkling her blue eyes at the Board over half-moon reading glasses, her white blouse, cameo, tweed suit, carnelian oval ring send welcome signals of reassurance, tradition, elegance to the Board whose collective expression seem to say: JUMPSUIT INDEED! She speaks with modest refinement, her English accent inspiring great confidence. The approval of some of the men shows more than professional interest in her good work done on behalf of the college.

I would be delighted Sarah. First, let me say I have been with Abington only three years, but I feel so attached to the college and to all of you who have given me such wonderful support and understanding.

Jessica's deferential manner allows the women to indulge in approving condescension, offsetting their repugnance for Goldrock. The Board settles comfortably into their cribs, rather chairs.

Now let me see....well I think I can say it has been a very good year, VERY good. Alumni contributions to the fund are up 35 percent and rate of participation seems to have improved dramatically. Our Legacy Fund has been especially important. Thanks to all of you, it has brought the college much needed support and secured long-term financial prospects. I expect my tour of alumni groups this month will inspire others to follow your sterling example. However, the support we are getting has little to do with me and most to do with the dedicated alumni who so treasure the Abington experience. Of course, tragically, we have lost several of our valued friends and supporters. We were especially saddened by the untimely death of dear Amelia Abernathy last month. Our hearts go out to Leonard Abernathy in his grief. And of course, lovely Betty Carlisle, Joan Bletchley Agnes Brady, Jan Amundsen, Christine Carleton, Judith Scales, Audrey Turner and Mary Fiske last year. But their legacy is green in our hearts as we face the future. Today I want to pay special tribute to our chair Marjorie Weatherby who just doubled her Legacy Trust Fund pledge to $4.5 million. Let's have a round of applause for Marjorie and her extraordinary generosity!

All rise and applaud, shout Bravo, then Speech! Speech! Marjorie, smiling complacent, acid, imposing, rises confident, given her years of public speaking as clubwoman and charity head, amply justified.

Well really. I am just pleased to contribute to what I consider the formative experience of my life.

John Witherspoon smiles as he recalls 19-year-old Marjorie's 'formative experience' in his arms in the garden at night as the orchestra played *Only Make Believe* at the Yale Senior Prom three decades ago.

Marjorie continues, to the responsive comments of the board.

We all wish to perpetuate the ORIGINAL spirit of Abington College. I have not always agreed with the PACE of change at Abington (gaining volume and authority)….nor have I ALWAYS favored expansion for expansion's sake….but I WILL always support growth within tradition! …. (imperious) And where we have departed from tradition, I sincerely HOPE, as I believe each of you does, that we may as soon as possible RESTORE the original conditions that made Abington the lovely memory it remains for all of us….

Right Marjorie, you tell'em!!!

….(furious) And FIRST on that agenda is to end co-education, if you can call it that, at the VERY earliest opportunity!!!!

Marjorie sits down to loud applause casting all her DAR, Wall Street, $80 million trust fund, Society of the Cincinnati weight behind her contemptuous look at Goldrock, who picks up the gauntlet Marjorie has thrown at her with relish, gaining steam from Board disapproval, and intensifying her Bronx accent and use of slang.

Look you guys. If I hadn't taken the college coed four years ago we wouldn't have any enrolment. We're lucky to get students whatever sex they are. The competition out there is fierce. The college is nearly a million bucks over budget this year for construction of the new student center and we've got to knuckle down to make up the difference. Of course, Jessica's activities are going to help bail us out as always.

Goldrock turns to Jessica, who again rises.

Marjorie expressed the feeling of us all who truly love Abington. As I begin another cross country trip to visit alumni I will bring that message. I am very optimistic that we can meet the deficit. In fact, I'm almost certain we can!

English professor Jason Amory, mid-career, untenured, father of three, with a recent mortgage incurred on the tenuous assumption of future promotion, was attempting to follow recent directions from Goldrock to ensure so far as possible the academic success of every student. Full tuition students were increasingly hard to attract and once found under no circumstances to be lost. The defensive battle cry, *Ils ne passeront pas!* so laudable in the trench war of 1916 now clearly inappropriate in the current academic battle to attract prosperous parents willing to spend money at Abington, graduating their modestly gifted children the price paid in return. Jason's class was regularly scheduled after lunch, 1:30 pm, but even a postprandial lapse in intellectual acumen could not account for the dismally modest effort of which students at best seemed capable, an effort that had to be taken seriously and appraised favorably lest these paying customers take off to more permissive venues. The subject today is Hamlet, rich source for misinterpretation.

So what motivation do you think underlies Hamlet's character? Yes, Alvin.

Like I see him as really sick, you know what I mean? Like why is he putting Ophelia down when his real grief is with the King? I think he's on something. Like what a trip, you know what I mean.

In-ter-est-ing. Yes, Belinda.

Like he's gay. You know. Ophelia's just a cover.

In-ter-est-ing. Yes, Alison.

Like he digs Gertrude, you know incest. She slept with him because the old King was sterile. He never got his head together after that.

In-ter-est-ing. Yes, Jacob.

Like HAMLET is an anagram for HALT ME. He's like looking for some dude to stop him from killing the King.

In-ter-est-ing.

Jessica pulls up to her Middlebury townhouse, gets out, and heads for the front door. On the doorstep is a large basket of two dozen yellow roses. She reads the card: Hope you like the color blue, it goes with your eyes. Love, Charles. She smiles and unlocks the front door. Inside, she goes to her desk in the living room and dials a Manchester England exchange. Her mother answers almost warily, as though the phone were invariably associated with bad news. Mrs. Hyde is quite attractive, but her beauty is submerged by a harried look. Her home is a dark brick 19th Century industrial row house, clean, decent and respectable, but there is an oppressive grayness that has worn her down over years of relative poverty. She looks at photos of Jessica 15 in a ballet tutu, Mr. Hyde in his railroad uniform, 10-year-old son Billy in soccer uniform, and Mandy age 23 in Greece with a boyfriend. Each photo evokes a distinct memory of love and concern.

Hul-lo?

Mum, it's me Jessica. How are you and dad?

Jessica luv. Oh, we're just fine. Dad is recovering from his operation very nicely.

That's good news. And how is Billy doing in school?

Last report undistinguished but he is holding his own. He owes you so much. Of course he is hopelessly ungrateful.

And Mandy?

Wild as ever. New boyfriend every two weeks. But a dear girl. Last I saw her she had a ring in her nose and black lipstick. Hardly recognized her. She may show up over there soon. Took off with her boyfriend to the States last week. Have no idea where she's got to.

You really suppose she'll turn up here?

Never can tell with Mandy. And you Jess, how are you?

Just fine. Remarkably so. The job is going very well. You wouldn't believe how much money there is over here. At this rate I'll be able to retire at 40. Well mum, I have to push off now. Just wanted to let you know I'll send another check end of this week.

You are an angel. Please come over this year if you can. Missed you last.

We'll see. Bye and luv to everybody.

Jessica hangs up, looking a bit worried at the prospect of her sister showing up.

Professor Pascal du Pin sur la Roche is conducting a counseling session in his office with Mary Poe, a Senior student. Daughter of a wealthy owner of Ford dealerships throughout New England, whose generous donations every year of her matriculation plus full tuition paid on time gave her, despite severely limited aptitude, traction in the academic course of her time at Abington. Not old money, not high-end professional money, but altogether real and ample money that exiguous times made more attractive and accommodation of her intellectual limitations more imperative.

Mary is physically exceptionally well endowed and not unattractive, an energetic participant in soccer, volleyball (always well attended by accessible men's colleges), and track, personable and well-liked by her fellow coeds given her generous nature and means to express it. Although no master of differential equations, more practical calculations were definitely not above her pay grade. We all at some time reach a fairly accurate appraisal of our capabilities. Not something we like to admit but definitely a factor in our calculations of advantages and disadvantages.

After her first semester, a disaster academically, Mary took a long and uncharacteristically shrewd look at possible means to repair the academic damage and secure a reasonably satisfactory progression to graduation, averting academic remedies, such as tutoring and extended study discipline, for which she was unsuited, incapable and disinclined. She had discovered her remarkable appeal on many occasions at Harvard, Yale, Princeton, Dartmouth frat parties, intercollegiate rivalry for dates with her sustained by a student grapevine account of her compliance on every occasion. By extension, she figured such appeal could work to more tangible advantage. Today was just another occasion to demonstrate her remedy which had proved successful in at least seven other student evaluations.

Pascal is seated at his desk set sideways with the right side open to the room. Mary is seated in an armchair at the side of the desk, wearing a very short thin jersey tank dress, at least one size too small, so tightly compressed that it is apparent she has nothing on underneath, her nipples nicely pressing outward in advance of her perfect 37C dashboard, the effects of such instrumentation she is now, at 21 years, fully aware and willing to deploy for all the advantages accruing thereto.

Pascal, atavistically French, is conflicted in his defense of la Belle Langue, in the face of threats to its integrity by the students of Abington, one of the worst offenders just happening to be seated very near him in his office late on a Tuesday afternoon. Being French, he is vain and tends to rate his sex appeal well above its market value. Throughout the session Mary slowly writhes in her chair showing to advantage varied arrangements of her body parts as he continues his increasingly uncertain remarks.

I'm afraid you did not do very well on the quiz, Miss Poe.

Oh, call me Mary.

Yes, well Mary.

Like I'm so worried. I haven't been able to sleep. I've got to pass French in order to graduate.

It's not too late. You have the aptitude.

I don't know what to do!

You just need a little application.

I'll do anything. Just tell me what to do and I'll do it!

I can recommend tapes.

Is there ANYTHING else I can do?

I suppose we could arrange tutorials.I

I've GOT to pass French to graduate.

They are not too expensive and…..

I'll do absolutely ANYTHING

He breaks off, as Mary thrusts her breasts outward turns her hip toward him. Overcome, all noble claims to defend la Belle Langue summarily suspended, he throws himself onto her, pulling her dress off as she raises her arms to make that easier. She is nude, delicious, willing, and irresistible.

Dieu, que tu est belle!!!!

A?

B?

A minus?

B plus?

OK!

Ahhhhhh…..

A technique used successfully with other professors over the four years of her matriculation, now guaranteeing graduation in the face of alternative legal liabilities too punitive to risk by academic careerists whose only prospect of future success is an unblemished record.

Jessica flew to La Guardia, got a cab to the Ritz Hotel, and at 7 pm took a cab to the Weatherby brownstone on 5th Avenue where Marjorie escorted her into the living room for cocktails.

I'll not conceal from you how much I abhor that person. She would never have been offered the Presidency had I been in charge. And to have taken the college co-educational just a year afterward. I hardly recognize the place.

That was before I arrived Mrs. Weatherby. I suppose it's part of the trend. So hard to keep up enrolment.

But look at the dreadful people they are getting. And the coed bathrooms. Really!

Charles Weatherby enters the room, well dressed, handsome, prosperous and confident.

Hello Jessica. The mob should be here soon.

Charles, I was just telling Jessica how much I dislike Madame Trotsky. We really must find a way to replace her.

I think Goldrock is kind of cute. Behind that butch exterior lurks a smart businesswoman. She knows how to play the politically correct card. After all she saved your precious college from certain oblivion.

That may not have been a favor. Besides I think Jessica will end up doing more than all the communist clap trap Goldmark dreams up. What in the world is she doing creating an African music department at Abington?

The front door chimes announce guests' arrival, the maid opens the door and voices of alumna and guests draw Marjorie to the hall to greet them. Weatherby moves close to Jessica and kisses her ear.

You look marvelous Jessica.

Oh Charles, I…..

She turns quickly away as Marjorie and a guest enter the parlor.

So good to see you Venable. Charles and I were just lamenting the state of Abington under Goldmark. Why is it Jewish social workers are taking over every decent college in America?

She wrote her doctoral thesis on the Attica prison revolt, good preparation for college administration from what I've seen lately.

The door chimes ring again, and more alumni and their spouses arrive and settle in the parlor, Jessica meeting each in turn, by now a familiar and welcome face. After initial greetings Marjorie calls them all to attention and explains that Jessica will provide an update on the latest news from Abington.

Thank you all for coming and special thanks to Marjorie and Charles for hosting this meeting, Abington is dear to our hearts, mine especially since I joined the College three years ago. If only I had been fortunate enough to attend Abington, but the next best thing is to help keep it the wonderful place it has been for all of you. As you know, our main appeal to alumna is to establish Legacy Trust Funds for the college which enjoy tax exempt income and ensure the financial stability of the college. This program ensures the future of Abington…..

Later during the party following her remarks Jessica stood near the fireplace when Venable Twist moved close to her and took her arm. He looked agitated.

Jessica, take this. Don't read it now.

He hands her an envelope, looks intently into her eyes, then quickly moves away. Surprised, Jessica puts the envelope in her purse and goes to join a group in the corner of the room. After the meeting she returns to her hotel suite, enters the bathroom to take a shower, begins to undress then stops. She remembers the envelope, takes it from her purse, and tears it open. A $500 bill and a letter with corporate letterhead **VENABLE INVESTMENT TRUST**.

Dear Jessica,
Here is a small gift just to repay the sheer joy I feel whenever I see you. Perhaps someday that will be often????
Your devoted,
Ven

To my beloved
When day has come and gone
And night imbues the air
And I am left alone
To misery and despair
I know that I shall never see,
Though mine are all your own,
Your eyes light up for love of me
However far or long I roam

She smiles, shakes her head in disbelief, puts the $500 bill in her purse. She walks to the desk in the living room, takes a leaf of hotel stationery and an envelope from the drawer. Sitting at the desk she writes quickly.

Dear Ven,
Your poem moved me to tears. So sensitive! I had
no idea of your feelings. I will donate your gift to the
Alumni Fund. Maybe someday......?
Jess

She addresses the envelope with the corporate address, stamps it, crumples up Venable's note, and throws it in the wastebasket, then takes her shower. Next morning she takes a cab to La Guardia and rolls her carryon to the boarding gate. She stops at a phone booth, drops eight quarters, and dials. An answering message comes on, she waits for the message tone and then speaks slowly: VERDI 2-7-4-3-M-E-W-5-8. She hangs up the phone, heads for the boarding gate, and on the way stops at 14-day storage boxes, inserts $50 bill in the pay slot, opens the door, puts a manila envelope in the box, closes the box, locks it, and puts the key in another manila letter envelope. She walks briskly to the boarding gate for her flight back to Abington, on the way she drops the envelope containing the storage box key in a mailbox.

The faculty room of Abington College was an eroded version of its original elegance. Worn cracked leather sofas and armchairs, oriental rug frayed to its warp, the pattern faded to an indistinct hint of its original splendor. Scratched and chipped tables and wooden cabinets, an old marble mantled fireplace, all redeemed by the warm autumnal early evening light coming through the leaded glass windows. Even the old streaked burgundy velvet curtains looked presentable. Goldrock and members of the faculty sipped drinks and discussed academic solvency, financial and scholarly, neither of which could be said to offer sanguine prospects.

We got an accreditation review next February. Chances aren't good. Nobody around here has written anything significant in years. The library is a joke. I better look for another job before the shit hits the fan.

Sarah, you are so grim. Abington has been around for more than 150 years. They can't just shut it down. (Pascal shrugged Gallically)

Should have been shut down years ago. Only reason they didn't last time was the Board hired me to turn this dump around. I got the money, but we got no depth.

The faculty members look hurt. Akim Toomumba felt insulted.

I resent that insinuation. I have an international reputation and can find work anywhere.

Nothin'personal Akim. But look at the situation. You do the African thing, Lee Anne does the Women's movement, Romero does third world. I got Leon Whitefeather part time on the Indian gig. I do alternative lifestyles. But we got no depth in the traditional stuff. What we got for science? A class called Numeracy for the Modern World. What the hell does that amount to? I got to start recruiting science talent as soon as I raise more cash. Hey, pass the nuts!

Jessica returned from grocery shopping Sunday morning and was putting groceries in the fridge when the phone rang. She goes to the kitchen phone near the back door.

Hello?

Jess, it's Mandy. I'm at the Greyhound bus station. Can you pick me up?

My God, Mandy! Yes of course, I'll come right over.

Jessica pulls up to the Greyhound station in her Jaguar. Mandy stands near the curb looking around vacantly. She wears a tie-died T-shirt, no bra, a miniskirt and sandals, quite a contrast to Jessica. She seems to look past the Jaguar, so Jessica calls out to her.

Mandy! Over here!

Mandy picks up her duffle bag and walks over to the car, laughing.

Jess, you look like the bloody fookin' Queen!

Next morning Mandy is seated at the kitchen table finishing breakfast. Her hair wet, just washed. Jessica comes down the stairs dressed for work. They obviously haven't got over yesterday's awkwardness, still a bit tentative, not sure what to expect on either side of the table.

I'll have to leave you for a while Mandy. You can take the Prius if you feel like going out. I'll be back around 5.

Don't fuss about me Jess. I could use a bit of down time. New York was awful. Bloody boyfriend ran off with someone at a party and took most of my money. Lucky I had enough to get here.

Yes….that was lucky. Well I'll be off now.

Jessica gets up and goes to the front door. She stops, turns, and smiles.

Give us a kiss, Mandy.

Mandy gets up, runs to the front door. For the first time they relax toward each other, hug and kiss warmly.

Thanks Jess. I mean this must be a real downer for you. My showing up. I'll bet you're scared to death what I will do.

Not at all Mandy, I'm delighted to see you. Why don't you try on some of my clothes. Find something you like to wear until we can go shopping for you. We'll go out to dinner tonight. OK?

Mandy goes upstairs to Jessica's bedroom. She turns on the radio. A classical music station playing a Mozart piano quartet. She turns the dial through scraps of news, talk show, a Poe Ford ad, to a hard rock station then turns the volume all the way up. She opens the closet and begins trying on suits, dresses, skirts, blouses, fixing her hair in different styles, even trying different makeup.

Late afternoon Jessica returns, puts mail on the small table at the foot of the stairs, and looks up to see Mandy descending. Transformed, elegantly dressed for dinner in a black sheath dress, a bit tighter fitting than it would be on Jessica, but all the more revealing of Mandy's attractive figure. She wears high heels, her hair held up on either side by silver barrettes, her makeup discrete but highlights the fine bones and great beauty of her face and pure blue eyes.

Mandy, you look absolutely gorgeous!

Jessica rushes to her, hugs her, looks at her. They hug each other laughing. Then Mandy begins to cry. Jessica also begins to cry and they kiss and hug each other.

Mandy sweet, I love you so much.

I'm not worth it Jess. I'm such a mess. I wish I were like you.

You're not a mess. You look absolutely beautiful. Tell you what. Tonight after dinner we'll go out on the town, such as it is. First dinner at Fenelon's then the Bennington Hotel for drinks and maybe some dancing. How's that sound?

You're a peach Jess. If you were a man I'd fook you right now on this rug.

That would be SO uncomfortable. Come on, help me dress.

The Bennington Hotel ballroom is crowded, mostly with tourists in for the Autumn foliage. Jessica and Mandy are seated in a banquette along the wall of the ballroom dance floor. Jessica wears an elegant blue dress similar to Mandy's black sheath. Both look ravishing and their sisterly similarity despite the six year difference in age is striking. The waiter comes up to their table and places in front of them two large glasses with red/white swizzle sticks and orange slices wedged on the edge of the glasses. He smiles broadly. These are the kind of women that make working Friday night worthwhile. Mandy surveys the room as Jessica takes a sip of her drink.

Jess, Navy 1 and Navy 2 look promising.

She indicates with her eyes two men in uniform, pilot wings on their tunics. Navy 1 catches her eye and gets up.

Uh oh, looks like the boarding party is about to arrive.

Navy 1 crosses the room and goes up to their table. He is irresistibly handsome and dashing as only a Navy uniform can be.

Officer Neal reporting for duty Miss. May I have the pleasure of this dance?

How cheeky the Navy is and always will be. Do you mind Jess, I'll see if this tub is seaworthy.

Navy 1 smiles, bows to Jessica, as he and Mandy leave for the dance floor, Navy 2 now approaches.

Miss, I can't leave you unattended. May I have this dance?

Jessica is beginning to feel very happy, even giddy. Mandy looks so beautiful, all her misgivings about her have melted away. Jessica has spent years devoted to building and protecting her career, calculating the effect of every move on her future. Tonight she feels young again.

Of course!

The couples dance, the combo changes tempo, plays everything from 30's swing to hard rock. Mandy and Navy 1 keep up, Jessica and Navy 2 follow suit. The combo sees they are terrific dancers and gets interested, playing progressively wilder dance music, breaks for drinks add fuel to the mix, much laughter as Mandy picks up steam. Jessica does too, but without the erotic abandon of her sister. Time flies, and around 1:45 the band plays a final riff and packs up, applauding the two couples, as the scattered remaining guests do also. The couples return breathing hard to Jessica and Mandy's table.

Marry me, I can't face living the rest of my life without a dance partner like you Mandy.

Drop anchor mate. I need to know more about your cargo before I ship out with the likes of you.

Persisting in this nautical jargon might have seemed tiresome or trite under different circumstances, but at this point it was received as amusing, contributing an appropriate lightness to slow down the growing potential earnestness of the latent relationship.

Mandy, it's nearly 2 o'clock. We'd best be getting back.

Oh no! Please! We don't want to stop now. Look let us treat you to breakfast. Please. We've never had such lovely company before.

Why don't we Jess? I'm famished. Or why not cook something at home? At least we'll be safely under our own roof when the buggers finally leave.

I'm not sure I have enough…

(Navy 1) Let's go shopping. Our treat. Waffles

(Navy 2) bacon,

(Navy 1) pancakes,

(Navy 2) ham,

(Navy 1) orange juice, eggs…

(Navy 2) and we'll cook while you two analyze our characters.

(Mandy) If we thought you had any character we wouldn't be going to breakfast with you.

They all smile in agreement, Jessica just a little apprehensive, and walk across the dance floor, in dance steps, toward the exit as the band's piano player cuts a final riff in appreciation. Back at Jessica's townhouse the four are finishing breakfast.

Not half bad. Why don't you two quit the Navy and open a diner and we'll come and have breakfast with you every day.

Mandy, I would willingly sacrifice career, duty and honor if I could see you at, and especially, before breakfast every remaining day of my life.

Admirable job. But we better clean up and end this delightful evening. Good heavens! It's after 4!

Jessica gets up. Navy 2 helps her collect the dishes and follows her into the kitchen, where they run water into the sink and begin washing the dishes momentarily not noticing that Mandy and Navy 1 are not helping. They are in the living room, kissing, she is still a little tipsy from the drinks earlier in the evening but certainly not to the point where she does not know what she is doing, and more to the point, what he is doing. She begins to respond eagerly to his kisses, relaxing and working her body against his. He becomes more ardent as she does this. Meanwhile in the kitchen Jessica is washing dishes and Navy 2 is drying and stacking them on the counter. He moves behind her and kisses her neck. She turns, surprised, and stands up slraight. All the charm of the evening suddenly passes, as she resumes her accustomed control.

No really, it has been such fun, but we must call it a night.

May I at least call you? I want so much to see you again.

Realizing that Mandy is not in the kitchen she smiles absently at Navy 2 and walks quickly back into the dining room. She sees Mandy and Navy 1 on the living room rug almost at the point of no return. She rushes over to them.

What the Hell do you think you're doing!

An undercurrent of rage and anger from her past, normally contained within a protective cover of carefulness, agreeableness, sobriety, breaks through with unmitigated ferocity.

Get off her at once!

She kicks Navy 1 on the thigh. Completely dazed, the couple part. He stands up. Mandy lies for a moment, flushed, looking blankly at Jessica as though not sure where she is. Jessica, having expended her rage and surprised at the violence of her reaction, becomes calm, not the calm of restored control but the calm of having faced something inside herself. She turns to Navy 1 and Navy 2 and says quietly.

You really must leave now. Please just go!

She takes their coats from the sofa and shoves them at Navy 2.

I'm terribly sorry Jessica….I got carried away… It's not what it looks like…I

(Gently firmly) Please! Just leave. I can't deal with any more.

They leave, Navy 1 in somewhat of a shambles, Navy 2 pulling him along and looking apologetically at Jessica before she closes the door. Jessica turns back to see Mandy, now standing and pulled together. They return to the dining room in silence. Mandy helps Jessica clear the remaining dishes from the table. They take them into the kitchen. They continue silent. Then Mandy speaks.

Sorry Jess, I think I just had too much to drink…. No that isn't true. I'm just easy. I like it.

Jessica goes up to Mandy, puts her arms around her, kisses her cheek. Mandy begins to cry.

Forget it, Mandy luv. We both need a good night's sleep. We will have forgotten all about this in the morning. But luv, you really should try saying NO once in a while. You may be amazed at the good results you can get.

Jessica smiles at Mandy. Mandy smiles, and they both begin to laugh. They hug each other, leave the kitchen arm in arm. They reach the bottom of the stairs. Mandy stops, turns and looks meaningfully at Jessica.

It occurs to me Jess, we're so unlike, if NO will work for me, maybe YES will work for you.

They both laugh and happily run up the stairs.

Sarah Goldrock, in her office seated in a swivel executive chair, wears a blue jumpsuit similar to the olive drab one she wore at the Board meeting. On the wall are photos documenting her professional life. Graduating from Gaucher College. Grad school at City College. Diplomas. A photo of her at Marx's tomb. News clipping of her arrest at city hall protesting. The desk and room are immaculate, free of clutter, almost as though unoccupied. Goldrock turns to look out the window at the commons. She hears a knock at the door and shouts.

It's open!

Jessica enters, closes the door. She goes to the leather armchair opposite the desk and sits down.

Morning Sarah. Enjoying the view?

A slender trace of irony enters the question.

Hi Jess. Yeah. Not one copulation or fellatio these last 5 minutes. Hey, I just wanted to find out how the New York trip went.

Not half bad. Got Mrs. Truehart to increase her Legacy Trust fund to $3 million. Probably what she spends on flowers every year. Mrs. Cassidy is thinking hard about increasing. I talked long and equally hard to her husband who seemed to be reaching meltdown before I left.

God how I hate those people. I suppose they trashed me all night. Ungrateful fuckers!

At their age they are not capable of do anything all night. But you were mentioned with varying degrees of affection.

I save their goddamn school from bankruptcy, with your help I should add, and they want to dump me first chance they get. Fuck their money. I came from a bunch of working slobs and got an education so I can do this for a living??? What a cosmic joke. How does the trip west look?

I'm shooting, as you would say, for $6 million in new Legacy Trust funds. About half in Chicago and the rest in San Francisco. Kramer, Biggs, Allenby, Bancroft, Bates, Zimmerman, Crosby look most likely.

I'm pulling a grant from Hong Kong. We'll sent up a symposium on Tiger economies of Asia. I need a drink.. Want one?

She pulls a fifth of scotch from the side drawer of her desk and two shot glasses.

No thanks Sarah. I have to make reservations. I'd end up in Zanzibar if I had anything to drink.

I hear ya. You could be making millions running a hedge fund with your charm. Wha'd you say you did before you got into this racket?

I came to the States as an au pair for the Summer. Italian family in New York. Eventually got a job at Barnard College working in admissions. Moved on to the alumni staff after that. The rest is history.

Family got money?

My father worked for the railroad in England. He had barely enough money to buy my ticket to New York, I had to scrounge pretty hard to make ends meet after that.

Working slob background. Good! Means you are an anarchist like me. If I could blow the whole bunch of them up I would.

She tosses back a shot of scotch and looks at the glass. Jessica smiles pleasantly, cryptically at Goldrock.

Mandy and Jessica are finishing lunch. Mandy is dressed in the outfit she arrived in. Jessica is in slacks and casual linen shirt, very elegant.

When do you expect to get back Jess?

I leave tomorrow morning. Return Sunday night. I'll call to let you know the exact time. Are you going to be all right Mandy?

You mean will I start fooking the postman? Yeah, I'll be all right.

That's not exactly what I meant. You have the most alarming way of putting things, Mandy. I tell you what. Let's go to town and buy some clothes for you. You're probably tired of wearing mine and something new might cheer you up.

Jessica gets up, kisses Mandy on the top of her head and starts clearing the dishes.

You're a bloody saint Jess. If you were a man I'd fook you right now on the rug.

They both laugh and finish clearing the table. Later that afternoon they are in an upscale dress shop. Several outfits are laying about. Mandy is trying on a slinky yellow flower print silk/cotton sleeveless dress that emphasizes her remarkable figure.

This isn't bad Jess. Sort of your basic streetwalker look.

It looks very interesting. Let's take it. We'll get this stuff home and you can pick an outfit for dinner. We'll go to Enrico's for Italian if you like.

Wonderful. I'll add five pounds and look as cheap as the house chianti in this thing.

We'll take all these, please.

The salesperson standing nearby collects the clothes. At the sales register she adds the bill and bags the clothes. Jessica hands her two $500 bills.

Smallest I have. Sorry.

Jessica arrived at O'Hare Airport at noon, took a cab to the Clarendon Hotel and checked in. In her suite she sat at the desk and wrote a note to her mother.

Dear Mum,
Just a note to tell you Mandy came to visit. She will stay with me for a while so there is nothing to worry about. Here is a little something to help out. I am headed to a meeting just now, so must run. Will write when I get back home.
Luv, Jess

She opens her checkbook and writes a check for $5000 to Mary Hyde, turns back to the register and deducts that amount. The balance is $32,680.

At 7:30 a chauffeured Bentley pulls up to the hotel entrance. The rear window slides down and Susan Blake calls out to Jessica. Jessica waves, smiles, and walks over the car. Inside the Bentley Susan mixes a drink. Jessica accepts a sherry.

Harley is so looking forward to seeing you again. I must say you are the only person from Abington we like anymore. That dreadful Goldrock was here last month and absolutely estranged everyone. But the college is doing so much better since you came. Maybe we can get to the point......

They pull up in front of an elegant north shore mansion. They get out and enter. Elegantly furnished interior where well-dressed somewhat petulant older alumna and their husbands nibble finger food and sip cocktails. A few punk students are present, sons and daughters of the alumna. Servers in tuxedos move about the room. Small clusters of alumna have intense conversations.

(Mary Crosby)....so Marjorie came out of the stall and there they were, two students engaged in fellatio, right in front of her. Well you can imagine....

(Betty Biggs)....they don't have any definite evidence apparently. Poor Joan, it's hard to believe she would lose control of her car like that....

(Alison Kramer)….she is so charming I could hardly refuse, especially since Bob virtually insisted…although I hardly know why he is so enamored with Abington all of a sudden….

(Emily Foxcroft)….how could Amelie have accidentally fallen from her penthouse. The balcony is nearly five feet high and she could hardly have lost her balance……

Susan Blake takes charge of the gathering and introduces Jessica.

Now everyone, if you will gather around… Jessica Hyde will talk to us about dear Abington…Let's welcome Jessica with a big hand!

All present applaud as Jessica with charming modesty begins her talk. There is a general expression of relief as she strokes their illusions about Abington College. Harley Blake, standing at the side of the room, looks especially rapt and adoring.

Thank you all for coming and special thanks to Susan and Harley for hosting this meeting….I wish I had been fortunate enough to attend Abington, but the next best thing is to help keep it the wonderful place it has been for all of you….Our main appeal is for alumna to join our Legacy Trust to ensure the financial future of Abington….

Repetition does not diminish the appeal of what we want to hear. The audience applauded, enraptured, notably Harley who later in the party moved up close to Jessica. He looks agitated.

Jessica, take this. Read it later. Let me know.

She puts the envelope in her purse and joins a group in the corner of the room. Later, in her hotel suite she dials home. Her message cuts in, no Mandy. She waits for the message tone and says:

Mandy. I'm at the Clarendon Hotel in Chicago. Phone is 312-476-2727. I'm in room 1043. If you can, call back before 8 tomorrow morning or I will try again to reach you. Luv you! Bye.

She goes toward the bedroom, then stops, remembers the envelope. She opens it and takes out a $500 bill and a sheet of notepaper with letterhead *Blake Barton Bloom Brokerage Incorporated*.

Adorable Jessica,
Here is a token of my admiration and some clumsy words to express it. I would gladly offer more. Someday??
Your devoted,
Hal

For Jessica
When night pervades the air
And light has come and gone
When I am left alone
Wandering in despair
I know that I shall never see
Though mine light up for you
And my heart be ever true
Your eyes light up for me.

Jessica smiles, shakes her head in disbelief, puts the $500 bill in her purse, takes a leaf of hotel stationary and an envelope from the desk drawer.

Dear Har,
Your poem moved me to tears. SO SENSITIVE! I had no idea of your feelings. I can't accept your generous gift. I will give it to the Alumni Fund. Maybe someday???
Jess

She addresses the envelope and stamps it, rumples up Harley's note and throws it in the waste basket. Later sitting in the living room drying her hair with a towel, she hears a soft knock at the door. It is nearly midnight, she looks puzzled and goes to the door.

Yes, what is it?

Room service.

I didn't order anything.

(She opens the door)

Charles!! What on earth are you doing here?

(Charles in bathrobe and slippers)

Lastly, I own the hotel. Thirdly, I was in Chicago on business. Secondly, I knew you were here for an alumni meeting. And primarily, I couldn't resist coming by to say hello.

While speaking he has entered the room and shut the door. He moves closer to her.

But the real reason is I adore you, absolutely adore you.

He bends down and gently kisses her. He kisses her again, and then again, holding her gently to himself.

But Charles, I....

He opens her robe and she lets it drop. He opens his robe and holds her closer to himself. He kisses her slowly and gently until she responds and puts her arms around him.

I love you

Yes!

Beyond reason

Yes!

Beyond life

Yes!

With all my heart

Yes!

Forever

Yes!

At the Manhattan Post Office a man with the words **Manhattan Maintenance Services** on the back of his jacket goes to the post office boxes. He opens one, takes out a stack of letters, locks the box and walks toward the exit. He riffles through the mail, gets to a manila envelope. He opens it and takes out a key, a ruby gold ring is visible on his little finger.

Jessica arrived at the St. Francis Hotel, checks in and goes to her room 1357. In the middle of the room is a large vase with two dozen yellow roses. She reads the card: *All my love, Charles.* She unpacks, takes a shower, and calls Dorothy McFaraday. Dorothy, a tall, large-boned henna-dyed aggressive Scot answers, stands on the balcony of her Sausalito home with a view of San Francisco Bay.

Hello Dorothy. Jessica here. I just arrived and thought I better call you for instructions.

Good you did. The alumni crowd meets at Melissa Truesdale's tonight. She's in the Marina. I can pick you up if you like. Say around 7? (Her questions always sounded more like orders given her peremptory manner of speaking)

Wonderful of you to go to so much trouble.

Probably. See you at 7.

Jessica hangs up then picks up the phone again and places a call to Vermont. The phone rings, the answering tape kicks in. Jessica waits for the tone:

Mandy. PLEASE call me here as soon as you can. St. Francis Hotel. Leave a message to let me know you are OK. Number here is 415-437-6161, Room 1357. PLEASE CALL!

Much later that evening, Jessica is with alumna in an elegant Mediterranean home in San Francisco Marina, with views of Golden Gate Bridge, Alcatraz, Sausalito, and Marin to the north. The ongoing party extends from the house to the back garden. Jessica stands by the fireplace. Dorothy McFaraday sidles up to her and whispers:

I'm on to your game.

Jessica, just for a split second looks frightened, then turns smiling to Dorothy.

Mrs. McFaraday you say the most alarming things.

You got a contract for 5 percent of all the money you take in. That's a hell of a deal given how well you've done.

But I believe that is the standard business arrangement. I had the same thing at Marysville College. Do you think it unfair?

Well, I suppose if you get results we should expect to pay. But you must be raking in at least $200,000 a year by now. The take last year was easily $5 million. Maybe I'll take that up with Goldrock next month.

Jessica looks uncomfortable at this abrupt challenge to her position, but is saved further awkwardness when Melissa Truesdale approaches, takes her by the arm and leads her to the center of the room to address the group.

Listen everybody. We want to welcome Jessica Hyde to our Northern California Alumni Association. She is an absolute treasure, in every sense of the word. In just three years she has put Abington on its feet financially, or at least got it off its knees. Jessica is going to bring us up to date on how dear Abington is faring. Let's give her a big hand!

(Jessica begins her stock speech) Thank you all so much for coming this evening. And special thanks to....

Later in the party Jessica stood near the refreshment table in the garden talking to a group of alumna. She feels a presence to her right and turns. George Truesdale stands looking at her with watery blue eyes.

Jessica, you look perfectly lovely. You must come see us MUCH more often. Please take this. Don't read it now. Wait until you get back to your hotel. (Looking at her more intently) It is truly wonderful to see you again.

Jessica got back to the St. Francis around midnight, tired with a severe headache. Too much smiling, too much sherry, too much alma mater. She needs a hot bath and a long night's sleep. She goes to the bathroom begins to draw her bath, then returns to the living room, both resigned and bemused to read what George has to say.

Dear Jessica,
I adore you. Here is a small gift just to repay the sheer joy of seeing you again. There is much more where that came from. Perhaps someday???
Your devoted,
GeeGee

Beloved
I know your eyes will never light
up for love of me
though mine like stars at night
do shine for thee.
When day has come and gone
and night is everywhere
I will be left alone
to misery and despair
wherever I may roam
because you are not there.

Jessica smiles, shakes her head, puts the $500 bill in her purse. She goes to the desk in the living room, takes out a sheet of hotel stationary and envelope, sits down and writes the address shown on the letterhead of the envelope, stamps it and writes:

Dear GeeGee,
Your poem moved me to tears. SO SENSITIVE! I had no idea of your feelings for me. I cannot accept your generous gift. I will give it to the Alumni Fund. Who knows? Maybe someday!
Jess

Marjorie Weatherby enters the dental office of Dr. Bradshaw in the Midtown Medical Building, Manhattan. She looks more irked than usual as Bradshaw and his dental assistant greet her with uncertain smiles, not sure what mood she might be in. As author of necessary but unwelcome pain on such visits, Bradshaw evokes very mixed feelings in his most temperamental (and prestigious) patient. An hour later she emerges dazed and no less irked from the dental chair, the left side of her jaw totally numb with Novocain. Bradshaw reassures her that the Novocain should wear off in an hour or so, but discomfort has little patience least of all in Marjorie's case.

Thooner the bether ith all I can thay.

Have a nice day Mrs. Weatherby. We'll see you for your cleaning appointment in December.

Marjorie opens the outer door and goes into the corridor. A workman is near the bank of elevators, on the back of his jacket the words Manhattan Maintenance Services. He is near an open elevator door which has a red down light on. Marjorie cries out peremptorily.

Boy, I thay boy, hold that elevather.

Yess'em missus.

She walks quickly around him, turns to look at him with annoyance, a look changed to outrage as she steps forward expectantly and drops from sight. The workman turns a master key as the doors shut behind her. A gold ruby ring is visible on his right hand as he moves quickly and quietly, unseen, toward the stair doors at the end of the hallway.

Jessica's noon flight to New York was delayed an hour so she had a sandwich at the SF airport. A good-looking man, probably Italian descent, came up to her table.

Little Bo Peep!!

Jessica looked up from her newspaper, startled. Says nothing.

You were a dancer at the Kit Kat Club in New York.

She continues to look at him startled, without answering.

You had the flower basket, shepherd's crook, pigtails, little girl dress. Remember? You drove us nuts!

Jessica still looks surprised, turns, searches for the waiter, waves him over.

Not possible. Must be someone else. I just got to the States yesterday. Excuse me, I have to catch my plane.

She gets up quickly, hands a $20 bill to the waiter who has just come over to her table, and runs off toward the exit. The man smiling, looks dumbfounded, turns to the waiter.

That's her. I'd know her anywhere.

The blue Jaguar pulls up to the townhouse. Jessica gets out, removes her TravelPro, goes up the steps, unlocks the door, and enters the living room.

Mandy!! I'm back!!

No reply. She closes the door, goes to the kitchen. No sign of cooking or dirty dishes. She looks concerned. Returns to the living room and runs upstairs. She goes down the hall to the guest room. She sees a pile of the clothes she bought for Mandy neatly folded on the bed. She sees a note on top of the pile, picks it up:

> Jess,
> I gotta be me as they say. Hitting the road for a while. I did take the flower print dress. May come in handy if I need to turn a few tricks for drug money. Just kidding!! Will call when I have news.
> Luv,
> Mandy

Jessica remains seated on the bed. She puts the note aside and takes up a folded jacket and skirt from the pile of Mandy's clothes. She hugs them to her and begins to cry, gently rocking back and forth.

Mandy, Mandy, Mandy, Mandy....

Jessica enters Goldrock's office, goes to the chair next to the desk. Goldrock is reading the New York Times. She swivels around.

Morning Jess. Hey check this out. (She hands the paper to Jessica)

PROMINENT SOCIALITE MISSING

Marjorie Eberhaupt Weatherby, wife of prominent investment banker Charles Weatherby, was reported missing after she did not return home from a dental appointment Wednesday afternoon. Doctor Bradshaw told reporters that she had had Novocain for a normal filling procedure. Both he and his dental assistant said Mrs. Weatherby appeared to be perfectly normal and was not suffering any unusual side effects. Police......

Astonishing! What could have happened to her?

That's the least of my problems. Take a gander at this poison pen letter.

She hands the letter to Jessica who reads as Goldrock summarizes the contents.

That bitch McFaraday intends to challenge your compensation package at the next board meeting. She thinks I'm overpaid too. They can stuff this job as far as I'm concerned. Christ! You've done more to bail out this dump than anyone and they begrudge a few bucks for your pains. I called this morning and explained that you have to pay all your expenses, including office, from the 5 percent.

As far as I'm concerned, both McFaraday and Weatherby can drop down an elevator shaft and good riddance.

Goldrock grins at Jessica. For a second Jessica looks wide eyed at Goldrock, then smiles an enigmatic smile.

Mandy and Navy 1 are in a motel off Highway 295 near Jacksonville Florida. Trucks and cars go roaring by at high speed. A thin white light from traffic arc lamps comes through a slightly parted curtain. A red neon sign goes on and off, adding garish intermittent color to the steamy atmosphere of the cheap hotel room. Mandy is standing near the foot of the bed. She is wearing the yellow flower print dress. Navy 1 on his knees runs his hands up and down her thighs and hips, his face buried in her golden triangle, groaning.

Please Mandy, please, please, please....

Mandy runs her fingers through his hair. She speaks in a thick voice, having difficulty restraining herself, but restraining herself nonetheless.

No! I'm saving myself for my husband.

Jessica enters a public phone booth downtown. She puts $2 dollars in quarters in the slot, waits for the tone, and then dials a 10-digit number. We hear a gruff voice say, *Leave Message*. At the tone, Jessica says:

VERDI 1-8-2-7-D-Mc-F-4-O.
I repeat: VERDI 1-8-2-7-D-Mc-F-4-O

She hangs up and leaves the booth.

Sarah Goldrock is seated at her desk reading the New York Times. She turns pages, reaches the middle of the front section. She picks up a shot glass of Dewers and is about to sip when she suddenly snorts and scatters scotch over the paper and her khaki jumpsuit.

SOCIALITE'S BODY FOUND IN ELEVATOR SHAFT
The body of Marjorie Weatherby, prominent socialite reported missing several weeks ago, has been found in the elevator shaft of the Midtown Medical Building. The police...

My prophetic soul!

In Doctor Bradshaw's office in the Midtown Medical Building, two officers are questioning him and his dental assistant. The Doctor and assistant look anxious. The officers look World-weary.

Officer 1: So doctor, can you think of anything at all suspicious or unusual on the day of her appointment?

I've tried to think back. But I spent nearly all my time at the dental chair. There wasn't anything to notice.

Officer 2: How about you miss. Did you see anything at all unusual?

She is unused to so much attention, takes any opportunity to prolong it. She has annoying distracting mannerisms, rattles on in an unpleasant high nasal voice and Bronx accent.

Oh, I've tried so hard to remember anything. It's so horrible falling down an elevator shaft like that. Let me think. I came to work at 8:30 as usual. Came up on that very same elevator. I stayed in the office until about 12:30, or was it 12:27? No, it may have been 12:32. Then I went out to get sandwiches for Dr. Bradshaw and myself. Must have been gone say 20 minutes. No more like 25. No, I'd estimate it was 27. Anyway, Mrs. Weatherby was due at 1:15. I came up on the other elevator. I went into the office.

The officers look at their watches. Then she almost cries out.

I think I DO remember something.

The men suddenly lean forward, close to her, hanging on her every word. She becomes confidential, almost whispering, excited.

I went into the office and ate lunch. Then around 1 o'clock Mrs. Weatherby showed up for her appointment. I took her in and helped Dr. Bradshaw with the filling. Shortly before the Doctor completed his work, I left and went into the reception area. I didn't see Mrs. Fenshaw, our next patient, so I went to the door to look into the corridor. Just as I opened the door Mrs. Fenshaw was about to open it from the other side. She came in and we greeted each other. I remember seeing a man in a service uniform near the elevators. Looked like he was working on one.

(Officer 1) Did you get a good look at him?

I can't be sure exactly what he looked like. His back was to me. I went inside with Mrs. Fenshaw and stayed in the office the rest of the day. Mrs. Weatherby left shortly after, but I didn't go to the door or look in the corridor again till I left for the day.

The officers, disappointed, sank back in their chairs, resume their World-weary expression.

(Officer 1, perfunctorily) You've been a great help miss. Old trick wearing a work uniform. Practically invisible. Question is, how did he get the elevator door open?

(Officer 2) Probably worked for an elevator repair company once. May have a master key. Well, we won't bother you any further. I'd like you to drop by the station to prepare a written statement miss, at your convenience.

The officers leave and walk toward the elevators.

(Officer 1) Dumb bitch couldn't identify him if he crawled into bed with her. Odds are one in a million we'll ever find the guy.

(Officer 2) Yeah, you can get away with murder nowadays.

Jessica, preoccupied, rushes down the commons sidewalk toward the parking lot and is about to open her car door when Pascal du Pin sur la Roche runs up to Jessica.

Jessica, I have seen so little of you lately. You look wonderful. Please take this. No. Don't read it now. Later. Au revoir!

She smiles, takes the envelope, tries to open her car door with the envelope in her hand. Then as if seeing it for the first time, she stops, tears it open, takes out a note and what appears to be a ticket. Bewildered, she reads the note.

Ma chere et belle Jessica,
Tu est belle comme le soleil, les fleurs. Je veut que tu sais comment je t'adore. Dedans tu trouvera un billet pour Samedi soir. J'espere que nous nous rencontrerons la. Mon amour est pour toujours.
Pascal.

A mon amour
Comme les nuages qui flotte
Dans léspace
Comme les fleurs qui jette couleurs
Pur comme la glace
J'érrais dans les bosquets
Tous perdu, désesperé
Jusqu'au jour que je te verrais
Ma belle reviendra.

Jessica looks at the ticket: ADMIT ONE ST MATHEW PASSION SATURDAY NOVEMBER 13.

Oh, for God's sake!!

She crumples the entire package into a ball and throws it into a nearby waste bin. She opens the car door, gets in, starts up, and spins wildly off toward town. Back home she takes her mail to her dining table and opens a large envelope and removes a note and a packet of airline tickets.

Dearest Jessica,
I'm free!!! Meet me at JFK on Friday so I can love and care for you forever.
Charles

She checks the tickets.

AIR FRANCE
Flight 109
JFK to LONDON
Friday, November 12

She smiles, goes upstairs in a daze of happiness. In her bedroom she begins to undress. She kicks off her shoes, unbuttons her blouse, takes it off. She passes the dresser and turns on the radio. It is set to a rock station at full volume. She reaches for the dial then withdraws her hand with a *'What the Hell'* look. She passes in front of the full length mirror on her closet door. Stops. She smiles, laughs. To the raw beat of the music from the radio she begins a striptease bump and grind. She slowly pushes down her skirt, steps out of it, picks it up, twirls it, and throws it at the mirror. She pulls down the straps of her slip one at a time, lets the slip drop and twirls it and throws it at the mirror. She unhooks her bra to the beat of the music, coyly removes it and throws it at the mirror. She shakes her breasts while pulling down her panties, steps out of them and twirls them, bump and grinding her pelvis as she throws them at the mirror.

In a flashback she sees herself at the Kit Kat Club on a raised platform facing a roomful of men and a few women at tables. Multicolored strobe lights play across the stage. A deafening amplified combo with obscene saxophone riffs and drum rolls plays *Little Bo Peep Has Lost Her Sheep*. Jessica wears a two-pigtail blonde wig. A flower basket is onstage to her right. She holds a Shepard's crook in her left hand. A pinafore dress lies on the floor in front of her. She twirls a skimpy red satin bra in her right hand. A group of rowdy young men at a table near the dance floor throw $20 bills at her as she bumps and grinds her tiny red g-string at them. The man nearest her looks like a younger version of the one who approached her at SF airport. At tables toward the back of the club are Mafia-like characters and their bullet-proof blond companions. Near the right wall under a red EXIT sign is Guido Panocidi, house bouncer. Jessica thrusts her pussy at the mirror, laughs heartily, and goes to draw her bath.

In a one-bedroom apartment in Manhattan, a swarthy stocky Italian opens the refrigerator in his kitchenette. He takes out a can of beer, shuts the door, and returns to the living room. He sits on the sofa, his shoulder holster and 38 magnum lying nearby. An end table has a lamp and a cork coaster with the words KIT KAT CLUB and a nude girl sitting on the edge of a Martini glass. He picks up the latest issue of COSA NOSTRA TIMES. The lead headline reads: *Exclusive Interview with Don Rigatoni: How to beat a wiretap.* He sips some beer, puts down the can on the cork coaster, pushes the message button of his telephone. He continues to read as he listens to the messages.

Guido. Tony. Tonight at 11.

Guido. Judy. Call me.

Mr. Panocidi, would you like to make $100,000 a year in your spare time and drive a Mercedes? Call 1-800-630-7600 for details.

He turns the page of the *COSA NOSTRA TIMES. Sicilian Don visits New York cousins.* The answering machine continues:

VERDI 1-8-2-7-D-Mc-F-4-O
Repeat
VERDI 1-8-2-7-D-Mc-F-4-O

Guido puts down the newspaper. There is an advertisement on the back page:

KIT KAT CLUB FOR ALL OCCASIONS
Don Ameliano Basta says:
'Great place. I take all my friends there.'

Guido gets up and goes to the bedroom. He opens the closet door and reaches up to the shelf. Five books of different colors are on the shelf. On coat hangers are a number of suits, sport jackets, slacks and several work uniforms with *Manhattan Maintenance Services*. Guido passes over the spines of the books, on his right little finger is a gold ruby ring. The books are titled:

RADCLIFFE ALUMNI DIRECTORY   MOZART
HARVARD ALUMNI DIRECTORY   BIZET
ABINGTON ALUMNI DIRECTORY   VERDI
WELLESLEY ALUMNI DIRECTORY   WAGNER
BRYN MAHR ALUMNI DIRECTORY PUCCINI

He takes down the Abington Alumni Directory, shuts the closet door and returns to the living room. He goes to the desk, gets a tablet and pen, and returns to the sofa. He rewinds the message tape to the beginning of the last message. He replays the message 1-8-2-7-D-Mc-F-4-0. He opens the directory, turns the pages to page 18, counts the lines down the page, stops at 27, Dorothy McFaraday. He writes down her name, address and phone number on the tablet. He closes the directory, puts it down on the sofa and resumes reading *COSA NOSTRA TIMES.*

Jessica al home seated at her desk, phone crooked between her shoulder and ear, talking to her mother in Manchester, simultaneously counting 20 $500 bills, squares them off and puts them in a manila envelope. She writes VERDI 1-8-2-7-D-Mc-F-4-0 on the envelope.

Yes mum, I have good news. I'll be visiting sooner than expected. No, nothing is wrong. Mandy? Oh she's fine. She left on a short holiday but will be calling me soon. Yes, I'll be sure to call when I get to London. Day after tomorrow. Yes. Ummm. Hugs and lots of love to you and dad and Billy. Yes, yes, of course, good bye.

She puts down the phone, licks the envelope, seals it. Picks up another smaller envelope and addresses it:

Allied Delivery Service
P.O. Box 1269
New York City, New York 20076

Jessica puts both envelopes in her purse. She goes to the hall, down the stairs, heads for the kitchen, sees that the mail has come, goes to the box and takes the mail. On her way to the kitchen she riffles through the mail, suddenly stops, throws all but one letter on the dining table and sits down. She quickly tears open the remaining letter, an anxious look on her face as she reads the letter from Mandy.

Mandy is sitting nude in an elegant hotel suite in Florida, writing the letter to Jessica. In the background, Navy 1 is sleeping on the bed.

Dear Jess,

Just a note to tell you the good news. I got a letter from Navy 1 the day you left. Decided to go to Florida to check him out. I did it your way. Saying NO did the trick! We were married three days ago. We've been in this hotel room for the past 48 hours getting to know each other. Got just a minute to write while he rests up. (Navy 1 turns on the bed) Looks like lover boy is waking up. Got to run but will call soon.

Sore but happy,

Mandy

Navy 1 wakes up and turns toward her smiling as Mandy finishes the letter. She gets up and walks toward the bed, nude.

Come on, sailor! I can't have any fun with that.

Back in Vermont, Jessica finishes reading the letter. She looks away amazed, smiles, smiles more broadly, smiles broader still, then begins to laugh very happily, joyfully.

Goldrock is seated at her desk, smoking a cigar, blowing smoke out the open window, a shot glass beside her. She is on the phone.

Yeah....yeah....yeah I know. Look, you're my agent not my mother....If this is such a good job why am I getting an ulcer?.... No way.....You got no idea....Forget it....Look, I need a job, West Coast preferred....Assistant Dean might be OK....How about Mills College?.....I can't take this much longer... Today I can claim a major turnaround....Next year they'll look under the rug and I'll be road kill....Do it George....My life depends on it.....Luv ya baby, bye....

Jessica is at JFK airport headed for the London boarding gate. On the way she stops at a 14-day storage box, puts $50 in the pay slot, and places a large manila envelope inside. She locks the door and puts the key in a small manila envelope, seals it and drops it in a mailbox. After boarding and takeoff, Jessica and Charles are seated in first class, champagne glasses in front of them. Charles reaches into his breast pocket and pulls out a ring case, takes out a 3-caret diamond surrounded by emeralds. Jessica extends her left hand. Charles puts the ring on her finger and kisses her. Jessica smiles enigmatically at the stewardess as the plane taxis for takeoff.

A week later it is 7:30 in the evening at the Ferry building in San Francisco, as passengers walk the ramp onto the ferry headed for Sausalito. En route, passengers stand at the railings enjoying the view of Golden Gate Bridge and the incomparable city skyline. Far aft, Dorothy McFaraday is also enjoying the wake and view of receding San Francisco. About half way across the Bay, the cool wind drives most passengers to the stateroom bar.

McFaraday, hardy, ornery and undaunted, remains aft. Suddenly, loud noise draws remaining outdoor passengers to the front of the boat to view roman candles and other fireworks for the Thanksgiving celebration. Dorothy stays put at the aft railing. A man in dark suit comes up behind her. He looks around and then kneels down as if to tie his shoe. He grabs her ankles and lifts her straight up, tossing her over the side.

He walks briskly back toward the stateroom bar. On the way the boat is rocking and he reaches for the railing.

He wears a ruby gold ring on his little finger. Aft toward San Francisco, Dorothy McFaraday bobs up and down in the choppy wake of the ferry, waving and shouting as the ferry chugs noisily, merrily and relentlessly into the night until no trace of Dorothy McFaraday remains to be seen or heard.

FINIS